the UnDeRDOgS

By Tracey West

Illustrated By Kyla May

SCHOLASTIC INC.

Copyright © 2021 by Scholastic Inc.

All rights reserved. Published by Scholastic Inc., *Publishers since 1920.* SCHOLASTIC and associated logos are trademarks and/or registered trademarks of Scholastic Inc.

The publisher does not have any control over and does not assume any responsibility for author or third-party websites or their content.

No part of this publication may be reproduced, stored in a retrieval system, or transmitted in any form or by any means, electronic, mechanical, photocopying, recording, or otherwise, without written permission of the publisher. For information regarding permission, write to Scholastic Inc., Attention: Permissions Department, 557 Broadway, New York, NY 10012.

This book is a work of fiction. Names, characters, places, and incidents are either the product of the author's imagination or are used fictitiously, and any resemblance to actual persons, living or dead, business establishments, events, or locales is entirely coincidental.

Library of Congress Cataloging-in-Publication Data available

ISBN 978-1-338-84522-8

10 9 8 7 6 5 4 3 2 1   22 23 24 25 26
Printed in the U.S.A.   40

This edition first printing April 2022
Book design by Jessica Meltzer

For my dog PeeWee,
my best friend for Seventeen years and the
inspiration for Peanut. —T. W.

I dedicate this Book to my Mum,
who taught me how to love dogs. —K. M.

Table of Contents

—

MEET THE UNDERDOGS

THE BEST OF BARKSDALE

1. ON YOUR BARK, GET SET, WOOF! 1

2. MY FUR! 9

3. A BUNCH OF RUNTS 25

4. WHAT'S THE POINT? 31

5. GRANNY'S PUP TALK 37

6. B-O-R-I-N-G 51

7. EMERGENCY! 61

8. R-R-R-READY OR NOT! 73

9. FOCUS, HARLEY! 85

10. YOU CAN DO IT, DUKE! 99

11. JUMP IN, PEANUT! 109

12. THE K-1 EXAM 117

13. THE FINAL SCORE 133

Betty's Biscuits

OUR BISCUITS ARE EVEN BETTER THAN CARLY'S COOKIES!

NOVA

She's super **EXCITED** to meet you!

DOWNTOWN BARKSDALE
THE **BEST** DOWNTOWN, PAWS DOWN!

MANDY & RANDY

These twins are the **BEST** at being snooty!

OLLIE

He has the **BEST** cool tricks!

CHEF WOLFGANG'S BISTRO

MS. FINELLA FINEFUR

She's the **BEST** principal!

CHAPTER 1

ON YOUR BARK, GET SET, WOOF!

Nova's three best friends stared at her, waiting for instructions.

Duke flexed his powerful muscles.

Peanut's whiskers twitched with excitement.

Harley's fluffy tail wagged back and forth.

"Okay, Team Comeback! Today is the day we practice for our Agility Exam!" Nova announced.

Harley frowned. "Is that why you asked us to come to the park today?"

"There's no point in practicing," Duke said.

"Yeah, we've failed this test every year the last three years," Peanut added.

Nova knew that Peanut was right. Each year, students at Barksdale Academy took nine K-9 exams. Nova and her friends had never passed a single test.

Failing had never bothered Nova before. She had always known that she and her friends were doing their best. But her three sisters were so good at everything—just like everyone else in Barksdale. And for once, Nova wanted to be good at something, too.

"I know," Nova said. "But this time's gonna be different. I can feel it from the tip of my nose to the tip of my tail. This is the year we're going to ace the test! Are you ready to practice?"

"Ready!" her friends cried.

Nova grinned. "Good. Now, on your bark, get set . . ."

SQUIRREL!!

Harley raced off toward the trees.

Nova stopped her stopwatch. "Harley, come back!"

Harley skidded to a stop. "Whoops! Sorry, Nova." She ran back to the starting line.

"Let's try this again, Team Comeback," Nova said. On your bark, get set . . ."

"WAIT!" Duke cried. "I think I hear a bear!"

"That's not a bear, it's a lawn mower!" Nova told him. "Mr. Poochwell is mowing his front lawn."

"Are you sure?" Duke asked. "That sounds like the growl of a bear. A big, scary bear with sharp claws."

"I'm sure," Nova said. "Let's try again. On your bark, get set . . ."

"EXCUSE ME," Peanut piped up, raising his paw. "But how exactly does this work? When you say 'on your bark,' does that mean *we* bark before we take off?"

"No," Nova said. "*I'm* the one who barks. I'll say, 'On your bark, get set,' and then I'll bark, and that's when you all start the agility course."

"But that doesn't make sense," Peanut said. "Shouldn't you say, 'on *my* bark'?"

"Peanut, you know how this works," Nova said. Then she saw that he was grinning.

"Yeah, I do," Peanut said. "Just messing around. Come on, let's start!"

"Are you sure nobody has anything else they want to say?" Nova asked. "Because I am going to start the count again, and this time I don't want anything to stop us."

"Okay," Nova said. "On your bark, get set . . ."
"NOVA!" Peanut yelled.
Nova sighed. "What is it, Peanut?"

Peanut pointed. "There's somebody on the course."
A small dog with feathery ears was sniffing around the agility course.

"It's Athena," Nova said. "I'll handle this. Then we're going to practice, and nothing is going to stop us!"

CHAPTER 2

MY FUR!

Nova walked up to the little dog on their course. Athena had her nose to the ground, sniffing. She was always investigating something.

"Hi, Athena," Nova said to her friend.

Athena didn't answer. She just kept sniffing.

Nova tapped her on the back. "Athena!"

Athena jumped. "Oh, Nova, it's you!"

"Yes, it's me," Nova said. She nodded over to Harley, Duke, and Peanut. "We're practicing for the agility test. So if you wouldn't mind—"

"You made this course yourself?" Athena interrupted. She looked around the park where Nova had

set up the practice course. There were obstacles made of empty milk jugs for the pups to zigzag around. There were ramps made of wood planks for them to climb. And there was even a Hula-Hoop hanging from a tree for them to jump through.

"Yes, I worked pretty hard on it," Nova answered proudly.

"Why not just use the agility course at Barksdale Academy?" Athena asked.

"We wanted some privacy," Nova answered. "And I'd appreciate it if you could—"

Athena nodded toward the hoop. "You know, Nova, there's a breeze blowing today. It could change the angle of the hoop, which would alter the trajectory of—"

"Athena, we really need to start practicing," Nova said. "Can we talk about this later?"

Athena shrugged. "Sure, Nova."

"All right, Team Comeback, let's try this again," Nova said. "On your bark, get set, **WOOF!**"

Harley, Duke, and Peanut took off as Nova's loud bark rang across the field. Harley quickly took the lead. She zigged and zagged around the milk jugs.

"GO, HARLEY!" Nova cheered. "You're making great time."

"Thanks, Nov—**SQUIRREL!**" Harley yelled. Once again, she ran off toward the trees.

"Harley, no!" Nova called after her.

Peanut made his way through the obstacle course next. He ran to the ramp and climbed up it. Then he slid down the other side.

WHEEE!

"Keep going, Peanut!" Nova cheered.

Peanut ran to the hoop. Then he skidded to a stop.

"I'm not jumping through that," he said.

"Why not?" Nova asked, but then she saw that Duke was sitting in front of the ramp. He wasn't moving.

"Duke, what's wrong?" Nova asked.

"It's too high," Duke replied.

"It's not that high," Nova replied.

Duke shook his head. "I am *not* going up there."

"Fine," Nova said. "Go around it for now."

"WILL DO!" Duke replied. He ran around the ramp and zoomed toward the hoop.

"Duke, do not go through that hoop!" Peanut warned.

"Why not?" Duke asked. "It's not as high as the ramp. I'm not afraid." He huffed and puffed as he ran toward the hoop.

"There's a big mud puddle on the other side," Peanut said. "And I am not about to get my fur dirty for some silly practice."

"HUH?" Duke asked. He couldn't hear Peanut over his own huffing and puffing. **"HERE I GO!"**

Duke jumped through the hoop.

SPLASH

He landed in the mud puddle. Mud splashed up and rained down. It got all over Peanut.

"MY FUR!" Peanut wailed.

Athena looked at Nova. "That's what I was trying to tell you," she said.

Harley ran up. "The squirrels in this park must be drinking rocket fuel for breakfast. I can't catch them!" she reported. Then she looked at Duke and Peanut. "What happened?"

"A mud puddle happened," Peanut said. "A stinky, smelly, nasty mud puddle. And Duke jumped right into it!"

Duke shook his head and his body. More mud flew off.

"Sorry, Peanut," he said.

Nova bounded over to them. She tried to run around the hoop, but she tripped through it instead.

SPLASH! She landed in the mud puddle, too.

"Puddle party!" Harley yelled. She jumped into the mud next to Nova.

Nova shook the mud from her fur as she climbed out of the puddle. "I'll admit, we just got off to a bumpy start," she told her friends. "But that's what practice is for—making mistakes! Let's get back to the starting line and try again. Go, Team Comeback!"

TEAM COMEBACK? MORE LIKE TEAM UNDERDOG!

Two perfectly primped dogs with freshly washed fur and long, curly ears were standing behind Nova.

"Mandy and Randy! How long have you two been watching?" Nova asked.

"Long enough to see that you and your team have no chance of passing the agility test," Mandy said.

"Yeah, no chance," echoed her twin brother, Randy.

"We do, too, have a chance!" Nova shot back.

"Statistically, there is a very small chance," Athena pointed out.

"You're not helping, Athena," Nova whispered, nudging her friend. Then her voice got louder. "You'll see, Mandy and Randy. This year we're going to practice really hard. We're going to ace all our K-9 exams. We might even win Best in Show!"

"HA!" Mandy laughed.

"YEAH, HA!" Randy laughed.

The twins started laughing so hard that they rolled onto their backs. They laughed and laughed and laughed.

Finally, they stopped and got back on their feet. The perfect pooches didn't have a speck of dirt or grass on them.

How do they do it? Nova wondered.

"That's pretty funny, Nova," Mandy said. "A bunch of underdogs becoming Best in Show? Here in Barksdale? That'll never happen."

"Yeah, never!" Randy said.

Then the twins jogged away.

"Can you believe those two?" Nova asked.

"Actually, I can," Duke replied. "Let's face it. We *are* underdogs, and underdogs never win!"

CHAPTER 3

A BUNCH OF RUNTS

Nova frowned. "That can't be true, Duke," she said. "I'm sure underdogs win sometimes . . . Don't they?"

Duke shook his head. "Nope. Not here in Barksdale, anyway. Here, everyone is the best at *something*. Everyone but us."

"Duke's right," Peanut said.

"Yeah, we're a mess," Harley agreed.

Athena cleared her throat. "I know I'm not technically a part of your team, Nova, but I think Duke, Peanut, and Harley have a point. The four of you started at Barksdale as a **BUNCH OF RUNTS**."

"Hey!" Peanut growled.

"I'm not being mean; I'm being factual," Athena explained. "Each of you is the smallest member of your family—the runt. Everyone at Barksdale Academy thinks you are underdogs because that's what you are. You remember what happened in our first year of school."

Nova groaned. "How could I forget?" she asked. Her mind drifted off into a . . .

FLASHBACK

Nova, Duke, Harley, and Peanut were the smallest pups in the whole school. Right away, everyone started to call them runts. And runts did not have a good reputation at Barksdale Academy.

"Runts may start out small, but they can learn to do big things," Principal Finefur said, and that was that. "Give them a chance."

But things went wrong right away.

THEY MADE A MESS! They ate like animals and chewed up their textbooks.

THEY DIDN'T BEHAVE! They barked all day and ran when they were supposed to walk.

AND THEY COULDN'T COMPETE! When it came time to take their K-9 exams, they were clueless. Everyone competing in the exams hoped to be named Best in Show at the end of the year. The competition was fierce! But Nova, Duke, Harley, and Peanut failed each exam:

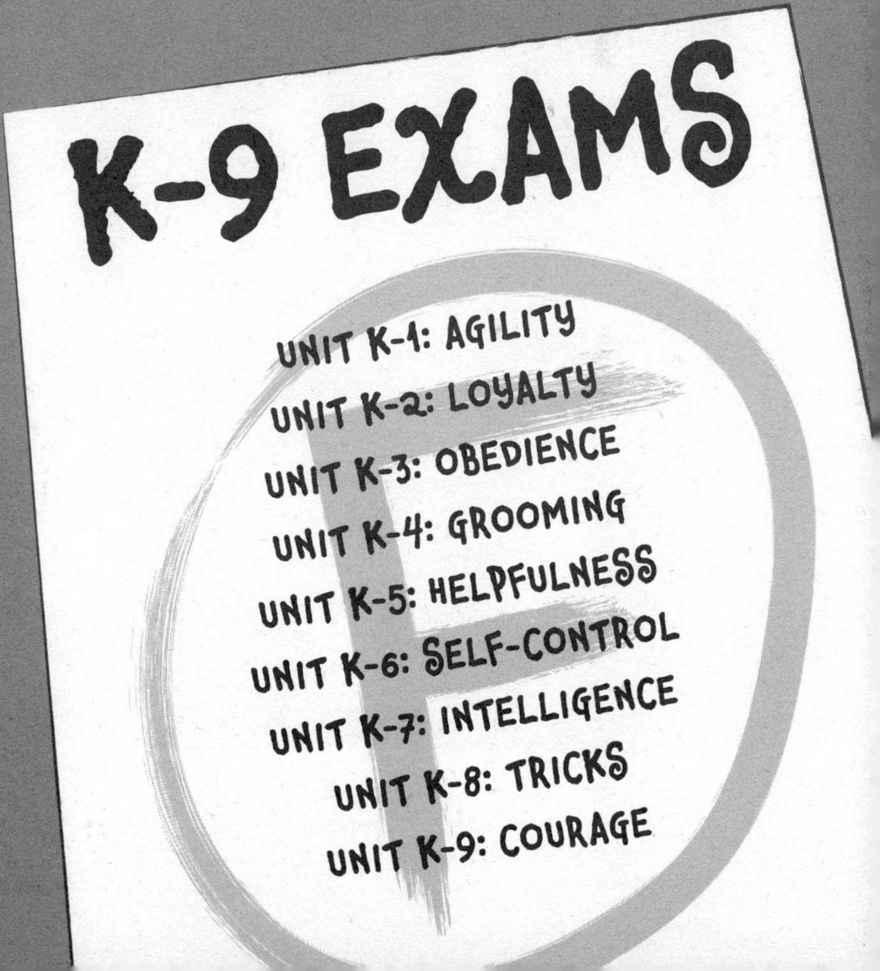

K-9 EXAMS

UNIT K-1: AGILITY

UNIT K-2: LOYALTY

UNIT K-3: OBEDIENCE

UNIT K-4: GROOMING

UNIT K-5: HELPFULNESS

UNIT K-6: SELF-CONTROL

UNIT K-7: INTELLIGENCE

UNIT K-8: TRICKS

UNIT K-9: COURAGE

Some of the other dogs laughed at them. Some of the other dogs made fun of them. But all of the other dogs started calling them **THE UNDERDOGS**.

CHAPTER 4

WHAT'S THE POINT?

"**H**ey, Nova, are you having a flashback?" Harley asked. "Your eyes have that glazed-over look."

"It's over," Nova said. "And yes, Athena, we *were* a mess when we first got to Barksdale Academy. When you're the runt of the litter, you get ignored. Nobody expects anything from you. So, when we came here, we didn't know much."

"Nothing at all, really," Athena pointed out.

"Hey!" Peanut said. "At least I knew how to groom myself. I wasn't totally hopeless in that test."

"Right. And everybody forgets how fast I am," Harley said, running in a circle.

"And how strong I am," Duke said.

"Exactly!" Nova said. "So what if we've never passed a single test? We've gotten a little better every year. And now is our chance to prove everybody wrong, once and for all."

UNDERDOGS CAN WIN!

"But practicing is boring," said Peanut.

"And no matter how hard we train, everyone else will still be better than us," Duke added. "What's the point?"

"Duke is right," Harley said. "Why can't we just keep being underdogs? It's not so bad."

"Come on, pups, we can do this!" Nova urged. "We're not runts anymore. We've grown up. We can do awesome things. And this is the year that we can show everyone just how awesome we are. I can feel it. That's why Team Comeback needs to get back out on that practice field!"

Peanut looked at his fur. "I need a bath first."

"And I don't see the point in training until we lower the height of that ramp," Duke said.

Nova turned to Harley. "What about you? You're with me, right?"

"I think—**SQUIRREL!**" Harley darted off toward the trees again.

Nova sighed. "I guess we can try to practice another day."

"Great! I'm off to the salon!" Peanut said, and he trotted off.

"I think I'll go see if I can order bear repellent online," Duke said, and he walked away, too.

Nova watched her friends leave. She shook her head. "That was a great practice course. We just needed more time! But they wouldn't even give it a chance."

"It was a nice attempt, Nova," Athena said. "But statistics don't lie. You pups are probably always going to be underdogs."

Nova frowned. "That doesn't seem fair."

Why can't I dream about being Best in Show, too, just like my sisters? she wondered. *Why do I always have to be an underdog?*

CHAPTER 5

GRANNY'S PUP TALK

Nova walked home.

Normally, when Nova went from one place to another, she didn't just walk. She ran. She bounded. She bolted. She sprinted. And when she was feeling full of confidence, she swaggered.

But today, Nova was not feeling full of confidence. She felt down, defeated, and dejected. So, she didn't run, or bound, or bolt, or sprint, or swagger. Instead, she walked very slowly, with her tail pointing toward the ground instead of wagging happily.

Nova walked through town. Normally, she would stop and sniff the air in front of Betty's Biscuits and try to guess what delicious flavor Betty was baking. But today, she didn't feel like it.

She walked past the Bubbles and Bows salon. Normally, she would go in and chat with Raven, the fur stylist, and catch up on all the gossip in Barksdale. But she didn't feel like doing that, either.

Nova didn't stop for a slice of peanut butter pizza at Chef Wolfgang's Bistro. She didn't stop to smell the roses at Fiona's Flower Shop. Instead, she made a left onto Bark Avenue, and then a right onto Dogwood Lane, and then she walked up to a yellow house with pretty flowers planted around it: the home of the Goldenfur family.

Nova's older sisters, Nina, Nadia, and Natasha, were playing catch on the lawn. They swiftly and gracefully raced around the yard, tossing a ball to one another.

Nina spotted Nova. **"CATCH, LITTLE SIS!"**

Nova looked up, startled. The ball came zooming toward her. She leaped up in the air. She caught the ball in her mouth . . . and then came crashing down on top of the prickly rose bush.

"OUCH!" Nova cried, and the ball fell from her mouth and rolled back toward her sisters.

"Better luck next time," Nina said.

"You'll get the hang of it someday," Nadia added with a nod.

"You okay?" Natasha asked.

Nova didn't answer her sister. She pulled the thorns out of her fur and trotted inside the house. She walked past the shelf that held her sisters' trophies.

BEST IN HELPFULNESS
Natasha Goldenfur

BEST IN AGILITY
Nina Goldenfur

BEST IN TRICKS
Nadia Goldenfur

Nova sat at the kitchen table and sighed. "I'll never be the best at anything."

Then she felt a soft paw on her cheek.

"What's the matter, my little Nova?"

"Nothing, Granny," Nova replied, but she sighed again.

Her grandmother sat next to her. "Come now, Nova, you're a sad pup if I ever saw one. If you'd like to tell me how you're feeling, I'll listen."

Granny Goldenfur gave great pup talks, and she was famous for her funny old sayings. She always said things like:

I'D RATHER HEAR A FUNNY TALE THAN HAVE A FLUFFY TAIL.

A BONE IN THE PAW IS BETTER THAN TWO BONES IN THE GARBAGE.

THE SQUEAKY MOUSE ALWAYS GETS CAUGHT BY THE CAT.

Her sayings sounded funny, but they always made sense when Granny said them.

Suddenly, the words started spilling out of Nova.

"I'll never be best at anything like Nina, Nadia, and Natasha!" Nova cried. "I don't want to fail the K-9 exams again this year. I want to pass them. Maybe I even want to be Best in Show! But my friends don't think we should even bother trying. What if they're right?"

"There's an old saying that practice makes a pup perfect," Granny Goldenfur said.

Nova nodded. "Exactly! That's why I want to practice for the K-9 exams."

"Well, I don't like that saying very much," Granny said, and Nova's eyes widened in surprise.

"What do you mean?" Nova asked.

"There's no point in practicing to be perfect," Granny replied. "Because I think you're already perfect the way you are, my little Nova."

Nova sighed. "No, I'm not. If I were perfect, I'd pass the K-9 exams."

Granny shook her head. "That's not the point. Stop worrying about the exams. It's okay to try, and to train, and to learn. But try to be the best Nova you can be. Don't worry about comparing yourself to anyone else."

Nova sat up a little straighter.

BE THE BEST NOVA I CAN BE. I LIKE THAT!

Granny Goldenfur patted her on the head. "Now, that's the Goldenfur spirit!"

Nova stood up. "Look out, Barksdale! I am going to try, and train, and study more than any pup you've ever seen!"

"That's not exactly what I meant," Granny said, but Nova had already bounded out the door.

CHAPTER 6

B-O-R-I-N-G

"GOOD MORNING!"

Nova ran up to Harley, Duke, and Peanut, wagging her tail.

Whap! Her tail wagged so hard that it knocked over Peanut.

Nova skidded to a stop. "Whoops! Sorry, Peanut!"

"No problem," he said, jumping back on his feet. "Your tail is soft and fluffy."

The four friends talked as they walked to school. A little fly buzzed around them. *Buzzzzzzzz . . .*

"Glad to see you're in a good mood," Duke said. "You looked kinda sad when we left the park yesterday."

"I was, but I'm not anymore!" she replied. "I'm on a mission. A mission to become the best Nova that I can be. And since we're a team, maybe you pups want to be the best Harley, the best Peanut, and the best Duke that you can be?"

"I honestly don't see how I can get any better," Peanut said.

"It's a cool idea, Nova, but—" Harley stopped talking, distracted by the fly.

Buzzz . . .

"What would we have to do?" Duke asked.

"Try, train, and study more than we ever have before," Nova replied. "I already started. This morning, I ran ten laps around the block before breakfast!"

Duke frowned. "I don't know. That sounds kind of hard."

"I need my beauty sleep," Peanut added.

Harley snapped back to attention. "I think an early morning run sounds great! That's when most of the birds are hopping around. And—**GOTCHA!**"

Harley jumped up, caught the fly in her mouth, and gulped it down.

Peanut stuck out his tongue. "Ew, Harley. That's gross! Why would you eat that?"

"Why wouldn't I? Sky raisins are delicious," Harley informed him.

"Sky raisins?" Peanut asked.

"Yeah, those tasty treats that fly around. That's what Pop calls them, anyway," she replied.

Duke whispered to Peanut, "Should we tell her?"

Peanut shook his head. "Nah. I'd hate to ruin her fun."

The four friends had reached the school.

"Anyway, you don't have to go on a run like I did," Nova said. "The whole idea is to just try to be your best. We can all do that in our first class this morning."

Peanut frowned. "History of Barksdale! But that class is so boring."

B-O-R-I-N-G!

History of Barksdale was taught by Ms. Finella Finefur, the principal of Barksdale Academy. She knew every single detail of Barksdale's history and loved to talk about it. And talk, and talk, and talk . . .

"I know it's boring, but we can all try to pay attention better," Nova said.

Harley nodded. "Sure, Nova. I can pay—ooh, look! Another sky raisin!"

Nova, Harley, Peanut, and Duke entered the school. Most students were hurrying through the halls, trying to get to class before the bell rang. Other students were still hanging around the lockers, chatting. A small group of pups had gathered around Mandy and Randy, as always.

"Good morning, Underdogs!" Mandy called out as the four friends walked past.

"Yeah, Underdogs!" Randy echoed.

Peanut stopped. "Hey, Randy. What's over there?" he asked, pointing.

Randy turned his head. "Where?"

"Ha!" Peanut laughed. "Made you look!"

Mandy rolled her eyes. "Very funny," she said in a voice that meant she didn't think it was funny at all.

"Why, thank you," Peanut replied.

Duke put a paw on his friend's shoulder. "Come on, Peanut. We've got to get to class."

"You're right! We're gonna be late!" Nova cried, and she raced forward. She zoomed down the main hall, made a right at the gym, and jumped through the doorway of room B-3.

As she sailed through the air, she realized she was probably going to crash into her desk. And crashing into desks was *not* doing her best.

Nova veered to the right and skidded to a stop along the floor just in time. She let out a big sigh of relief.

Crash averted! she thought, and then she gave herself a pup talk. *Keep it up, Nova. Keep being your best!*

CHAPTER 7

EMERGENCY!

The other students entered the classroom. Besides Harley, Duke, and Peanut, Athena, Randy, and Mandy were also in the class. So was Nova's friend Ollie. He rolled into class using the wheels strapped to his back legs. He spun in a circle and then slid up to the desk next to Nova.

The bell rang, and Principal Finefur trotted in. She was smaller than most of her students, with long, straight fur cascading down her sides. It brushed against the floor as she walked. She stood in front of the classroom and adjusted her eyeglasses with her paw.

"Good morning, students!" she greeted them.

"GOOD MORNING, PRINCIPAL FINEFUR!"

"I have an exciting lecture planned for you this morning," the principal continued. "As we learned yesterday, there are 317 different streets in Barksdale. Each one of them has a different name. How did they get those names? I am about to tell you. First, Main Street. It used to be called Weimaraner Road, but nobody could ever get the spelling right. So, the town held a meeting . . ."

Nova tried to pay attention. She really did. But Peanut was right. Principal Finefur's lectures could be B-O-R-I-N-G.

By the time Principal Finefur got to talking about Terrier Terrace, Peanut tossed something at Nova. She looked to see a folded-up note on her desk. She opened it.

Nova wanted to laugh, but she held it in. She needed to focus so she could do her best in class. *Is everyone else having trouble focusing, too?* she wondered.

She turned and looked at Duke. He was asleep, and drool dripped from his mouth. *Drip* . . . *drip* . . . *drip* . . .

Next to Duke, Harley was staring at the open window. A squirrel nibbled on a nut in a nearby tree, and Harley's whiskers twitched.

Nova sniffed the air coming through the window and smelled . . . roses. *The rose bush by the front pathway must have bloomed this morning,* she thought.

She sniffed again and smelled . . . a mouse. *It's definitely a mouse looking through the garbage can outside. A combination of fur and stale cheese.*

She sniffed a third time and smelled something farther away . . . smoke. *Wood smoke,* she thought. *Coming from Main Street . . . like something is on fire!*

BAM! She jumped over her desk, knocking it over. She bolted for the classroom door.

BAM! She toppled the books on Athena's desk and tipped over the wastebasket. Then she raced through the halls toward the front entrance.

BAM! She knocked over a mop bucket, and the water sloshed all over the floor.

BAM! She bumped into Coach Houndstooth, who was carrying a bag to the gym. He dropped it, and the balls inside spilled out and rolled everywhere.

Nova charged through the door and ran to Main Street, jumping over bushes and rocks and fire hydrants to get there as fast as she could. She could see plumes of gray smoke in the blue sky the closer she got. She followed her nose to the source of the smell, and stopped in front of Chef Wolfgang's Bistro. The chef was outside.

"Chef Wolfgang!" Nova cried, racing up to him. "Your restaurant's on fire!"

Chef Wolfgang smiled. "Oh, Nova, don't worry. The bistro isn't on fire. I just installed a brand-new outdoor pizza oven and fired it up. Let me show you."

Nova followed him to the side of the building, where wood burned in a brick oven. Smoke floated out of the oven's chimney and into the sky. Nova's mouth opened, and she stared at it.

"I . . . I'm glad your restaurant's not on fire," she finally said.

"Thanks for trying to warn me," Chef Wolfgang said. "Now, shouldn't you be in school?"

School! Nova thought, and her race to the bistro came back to her. The knocked-over books, and trash, and mop water, and balls . . .

Nova sighed. "Yes, I'd better get back."

"Come back later for a free slice of pizza!" Chef Wolfgang called after her as she ran.

When Nova returned to Barksdale Academy, Principal Finefur and the rest of her classmates were in front of the school.

"Nova, is everything all right?" the principal asked.

Nova nodded. "Yup," she said. "Turns out it was just Chef Wolfgang's new pizza oven."

Some of the pups started to giggle.

"You ran out of here for a pizza emergency?" Mandy asked. "What was the matter? Not enough cheese?"

Randy snorted. "Yeah, not enough cheese?"

Nova's eyes filled with tears, and she ran into the building.

What good is being the best Nova I can be if that just means I'm the best at making a mess?

CHAPTER 8

R-R-R-READY OR NOT!

"**A**ll right, pups! Five laps around the track!" Coach Houndstooth barked.

Ace Swiftrunner led the pack. Ace was the fastest dog in the school and the best at everything he tried. He was especially good at being nice. When everyone else had made fun of the Underdogs, Ace hadn't joined in. Instead, he had become their friend.

73

Behind Ace was Ollie, zipping along on his wheels. Ollie had moved to Barksdale a year ago. Ace and Ollie had quickly become besties, maybe because Ollie was good at everything, too.

The rest of the students jogged along at their own speed. And all the way at the back of the pack, Nova moped along.

Mandy and Randy hung back until she caught up.

"Hey, Nova, I hear there's a **HAMBURGER EMERGENCY** in town," Mandy teased.

Nova sighed. "Very funny, Mandy."

"And I heard there was a flood emergency, too," Randy added.

Mandy frowned at her brother. "That's not how it works. It has to be food or it's not funny."

"Uh, okay," Randy said. "Nova, I hear there's a **BANANA EMERGENCY**."

Mandy shrugged. "Better. Anyway, Nova, you'd better be careful running laps in case you knock something over!"

Harley, Duke, and Peanut jogged back to Nova. **"LEAVE NOVA ALONE, MANDY AND RANDY!"** Harley said. "She was just trying to be helpful."

Peanut nodded. "Yeah, she can't help it if she knocked over a desk, and the garbage, and books, and a bucket of water, and—"

Duke nudged his friend. "You're not helping, little dude."

Mandy and Randy raised their snouts in the air.

"Good luck, Underdogs!" Mandy said as they jogged away.

"Yeah, you'll need it!" Randy added.

After everyone ran their laps, they gathered in front of Coach Houndstooth.

"Today, I've got some tips for you for the agility course," he began. "I know for some of you the course will be r-r-r-ruff, but today I'll show you how to get r-r-r-ready! Ace, come on up here and help me demonstrate."

The spotted dog bounded over to Coach Houndstooth. "Ready, Coach!"

"Ace, weave through those orange cones," Coach ordered. He started his stopwatch.

Ace sprang into action, weaving through a line of orange cones set up on the athletic field behind the school.

Harley leaned toward Nova. "I can do that, too," she whispered, and then her eyes fixed on a stand of trees on the side of the field. "I'm just as fast as— **SQUIRREL!**" And she raced away.

"Notice how Ace gets power from his back legs, but changes direction with his front legs," Coach Houndstooth pointed out. "Ace, the r-r-r-ramp!"

The athletic dog raced to the ramp and reached the top in one swift move, then jumped down the other side.

Duke shivered. "That ramp is so high!"

"Once again, Ace is getting his power from his back legs," Coach Houndstooth explained. "Next, the hoop!"

Ace sailed through the hoop, landing gracefully on his four feet.

"Notice how he's controlling his muscles, even when he's midair," Coach Houndstooth said. "That's the key to keeping your balance. Great job, Ace!"

Nova sighed. "He's amazing. I don't think I could ever make a smooth landing like that."

Ace trotted back to Coach Houndstooth.

"Look how muddy his paws are after that!" Peanut sniffed. "Why does agility training have to be so messy?"

"To help prep for your agility exam, let's work on strengthening those back legs," Coach announced. "Line up and give me some squats!"

Nova watched her friends as they lined up for the exercise and thought about the last few days.

Maybe my friends are right, she thought. *What's the point of training for the agility exam if we're not cut out for it? I can't run without crashing into everything. Harley loses concentration every time she sees a squirrel. Duke is afraid of heights. And Peanut won't do anything that's too messy. Unless there's some way to fix all this . . .*

Maybe there is*!*

After school, Nova spoke to Harley, Duke, and Peanut. "Are you pups ready for another training session with me?" she asked.

"Sure, Nova!" Harley replied.

"If it makes you happy," Duke said.

"Not really," Peanut answered, and Duke growled at him. "I mean, sure!"

Nova ran around them, excited. "Great! Because I think I know how to solve all our problems!"

CHAPTER 9

FOCUS, HARLEY!

"One . . . two . . . three . . ."

Nova counted as she slowly walked across her backyard the next day. Granny Goldenfur was digging in the garden when she noticed Nova walk by.

"Nova, why is there a plate of biscuits on your head?" Granny asked.

"I'm practicing," Nova replied. "I can't do my best in the agility exam because I'm always crashing into things. I need to learn how to control my movements. Four . . . five . . . six . . ."

Granny nodded. "I suppose that's one way to do it," she said. "But I like the way you move. You're fast, and you're always smiling, and you look like you're having fun."

"Usually I am," Nova said. "But having fun is not going to help me pass the K-1 agility test. Seven . . . eight . . . nine . . ."

"Maybe not," Granny agreed. "But you know what I always say. I'd rather have a good time than be on time."

"What does that have to do with me?" Nova asked. "Ten . . . eleven . . . whoa!"

Nova tripped on Granny's rake. The plate of biscuits flew off her head. Biscuits rained down everywhere. Granny jumped and gulped one down. She caught the rest in her paws.

"I make a mess out of everything!" Nova cried, flopping down on the grass.

"No use crying over spilled biscuits," Granny said, and she handed Nova one. "Now, would you like to help me plant these daisies?"

"I wish I could, but I've got to meet my friends in the park," Nova told her. **"SEE YOU LATER, GRANNY!"**

Nova grabbed her backpack and ran off.

Maybe my practice didn't turn out so great, she thought. *But wait until my friends see what I've got planned for them!*

Harley, Duke, and Peanut were waiting for Nova when she arrived.

"We set up the course, just like you asked," Harley said, nodding toward the milk jugs, the ramp, and the hoop. "Should we head to the starting line?"

Nova shook her shaggy head. "Nope. New plan today. We're going to work on making each of us better, one at a time. Harley, you're up first."

"YIPPEE!" Harley cheered, running in a circle. "What do I have to do?"

"Just wait here for now," Nova told her. "Duke and Peanut, follow me."

The two dogs followed Nova behind a bush. She took two furry costumes out of her backpack.

"What's this?" Duke asked.

"I need you two to dress up like squirrels," Nova explained. "So we can help Harley learn how to concentrate."

Duke frowned. "Are you sure that's going to work?"

"I'll do it!" Peanut cried. He slipped the costume on and began to strut back and forth. "I'm a squirrel supermodel—work it!"

Duke sighed and put on his own costume. Peanut took one look at him, dropped to the ground, and began rolling with laughter. "**HA HA HA HA HA HA HA!** Duke the squirrel! This is great!"

Duke's eyes narrowed. "You're wearing the same thing, Peanut."

"I know, but I'm squirrel-sized," Peanut pointed out. "You look like a giant squirrel. Mega Squirrel! Squirrelsaurus! Squirrelzilla!"

Duke chuckled and started stomping his feet.

GIVE ME ALL THE NUTS OR I WILL DESTROY YOUR CITY!

"All right, enough joking around," Nova instructed. "Wait here. I'm going to give Harley a pup talk. When she starts on the course, run out and try to distract her."

Peanut saluted. "Aye, aye, Squirrel Boss!"

Nova rolled her eyes and trotted over to Harley.

"Okay, Harley," she began. "I want you to run the course. There might be some squirrels who will—"

"**SQUIRRELS?** Where?" Harley asked.

"Nowhere—not yet, anyway," Nova continued. "Harley, when you see a—a furry, nut-eating creature— then I want you to focus. When your brain says '**SQUIRREL,**' I want you to think, '**FINISH.**' Got it?"

Harley nodded. "Finish. Finish. Finish. Got it."

"On your bark, get set, **GO**!" Nova yelled.

Harley took off running. She zigzagged through the milk bottles.

"Duke, now!" Nova yelled.

Duke ran out of the bushes. "Nothing to see here but me, a hungry squirrel looking for acorns. I really, really love acorns."

Harley stopped. She looked at Duke.

"Harley, finish!" Nova yelled.

"Finish. Finish. Finish," Harley said, and she kept running.

"Peanut, now!" Nova yelled.

Peanut ran out in front of the ramp. "Look at me! I'm a squirrel with tiny ears and a ridiculously fluffy tail!"

Harley paused on top of the ramp. Her right eye began to twitch.

"Harley, finish!" Nova cried.

Harley ran up the ramp. Peanut moved to the side.

"Peanut, Duke, go to the finish line!" Nova instructed.

Duke and Peanut ran to the finish line as Harley continued the course.

"Finish, Harley!" Nova cheered. "You can do it!"

"Finish. Finish. Finish," Harley chanted as she neared the finish line. Duke and Peanut stood next to each other, right in front of it.

Harley's eye twitched again. Her tail wagged.

"Finish. Finish. **SQUIRREL!**" she shouted, and she lunged after Duke and Peanut. The two dogs raced to get away from her.

"Harley, it's Peanut, your friend!" Peanut cried as Harley snapped at his furry tail. "Your one-hundo-percent canine friend who is NOT a squirrel."

Harley chased Duke and Peanut across the park, and Nova sighed.

"Stop, Harley! We need to keep practicing!" Nova yelled as she ran after her friends.

My plan for Harley didn't work. But I won't give up!

CHAPTER 10

YOU CAN DO IT, DUKE!

Harley caught up to Duke first. She pinned him to the ground.

"Harley, snap out of it. It's me, Duke!" he wailed.

Harley stopped. She sniffed.

"Oh, hi, Duke," she said, jumping off him. "Why are you dressed like a squirrel?"

"It was Nova's idea," he replied, getting to his feet.

Peanut came around, holding the squirrel costume in his mouth. He dropped it on the grass.

"Thanks a lot, Nova," Peanut said. "Harley almost ate us for lunch!"

"I don't *eat* squirrels," Harley corrected him. "I just like to chase them. And catch them. And play with them. And nibble on their furry tails. And . . ." Her eyes glazed over as she thought about it.

"All right, so maybe that wasn't the best idea," Nova admitted. "But you almost had it, Harley. You almost crossed the finish line."

"I guess you're right, Nova," Harley said. "I'll do better next—**SQUIRREL!**"

She raced off to chase a real squirrel. Nova looked at Duke and Peanut.

"Okay, which one of you wants to go next?"

Duke looked down at the ground. Peanut whistled and looked at the sky.

"Come on, it won't be so bad," Nova said. "Follow me to the bleachers. Duke, you're up!"

Duke and Peanut exchanged worried looks, but they followed their friend to the park's athletic field. Metal bleachers, ten rows high, were there for fans to watch Barksdale competitions.

"Duke, we're going to work on your fear of heights," Nova announced.

Duke gulped and looked at the bleachers. "Really?"

"We'll take it slow," Nova promised. "Start by stepping onto the first row of the bleachers."

"Really? Way up there?" Duke asked.

"Dude, that step is as tall as you are," Peanut pointed out.

Duke took a deep breath. "Okay, I got this."

He put one paw on the first row. Then another. Then he hoisted himself up.

"I'm doing it," he said. Then he looked down. "Oh no. I'm getting dizzy!"

"Close your eyes, Duke," Nova urged him. "Take some deep breaths. Then open them again. You'll see that you're not so high up."

Duke closed his eyes and took deep breaths. He opened them.

"Okay," he said. "This isn't so bad. The ground isn't too far below me. And you and Peanut are right there."

"We sure are, buddy!" Peanut said.

Nova wagged her tail. "Great job, Duke! Now climb up to the next row."

Duke eyed the second row. "Hmm. Maybe we could, you know, take this even more slowly? I could come back tomorrow and start fresh."

Nova didn't want her friend to give up. "Give it a try now. You can do it, Duke!"

"Go, Duke!" Peanut cheered.

Duke slowly climbed up to the second row. He closed his eyes. He took some deep breaths. "Hey, this isn't so bad," he said.

Nova smiled. "See? I told you. Now, go to the third row."

Duke stepped onto the third row of the bleachers. He closed his eyes. He took some deep breaths. While he did that, a little bird flew onto the bleachers next to him. Duke opened his eyes.

"Okay, I'm—wait, what's this bird doing here?! I must be flying in the sky! I'm too high. **TOO HIGH!**"

"It's okay, Duke!" Nova cried. "You're not very high at all. The bird just flew *down* from the sky."

Suddenly, the bird flapped its wings. Duke panicked and ran down the bleachers. He flopped onto the ground, landing right on top of Peanut.

"Sorry, little dude," Duke said.

"That's okay," Peanut replied, squeezing out from under him. "I've always wondered what it felt like to be a pancake."

Harley ran up. "What did I miss?"

Nova focused on the positive. "Duke climbed up to the third row of the bleachers! It was awesome."

"Yeah, until he saw a bird and thought he was high in the sky and freaked out," Peanut muttered.

Nova spun around. "Good news, Peanut. It's your turn next! I think you're going to love what I have planned."

Peanut shook his head. "Oh noooo, Nova. Whatever you've got in mind, I am not going to do it!"

CHAPTER 11

JUMP IN, PEANUT!

"**I**f I had to climb into the sky, then you have to do your thing, Peanut," Duke said as they followed Nova across the park.

"I'm not making any promises," Peanut replied. "I have a feeling that what Nova has planned for me is much worse."

Nova led them to the park caretaker's shed, where Athena was waiting for them. She was holding a hose and soaking a patch of dirt with water.

Harley's ears twitched with excitement. "Ooh, I love a good mud puddle!"

Athena stopped the hose. "I think it's at just the right consistency, Nova. Wet enough to splash around in, but not so wet that the mud won't stick to your fur."

Nova grinned. "Excellent!"

Peanut began to slowly back away.

"You don't have to jump in right away, Peanut," Nova explained. "But I thought if you saw how much fun getting messy was, you might change your mind. Now I'll just jump in and—"

Harley leapt in the air and landed in the mud puddle first. Mud splashed out, and Peanut took another step back.

"You don't know what you're missing, Peanut!" Harley called out. "This mud is super squishy and just the right temperature. It's awesome!"

Peanut shook his head. "No, thank you."

Duke stepped into the puddle and started to stomp around. "Just stick your feet in, little dude. It's fun."

"Thanks, but no thanks," Peanut replied.

Nova jumped in next. She rolled around in the mud, then got back on her feet and shook her fur, sending mud particles flying everywhere.

"It feels great, Peanut!" Nova said. "And when you're all done, you just wash off and you're clean again."

But Peanut did not budge. "No to the one hundredth power, no!"

Nova sighed. "I don't understand, Peanut. Why won't you just give it a try? Don't you want us to pass the agility exam?"

"There's got to be some other way!" Peanut insisted. "I do **NOT** like being messy."

Then the little dog ran away.

"Peanut, it's okay! Come back!" Nova called out.

Nova, Harley, and Duke sat in the mud puddle sadly. After a moment, Nova climbed out.

"Please hose me off, Athena," she said.

"Sure," Athena replied, and she began to spray Nova with water. "Poor Peanut. It's a shame the school isn't more agile when it comes to the agility exam."

"What do you mean?" Nova asked.

"Well, 'agility' means to move quickly and easily. It means you can change direction when you're running without slowing down. Maybe it's time the test changed direction so that more of us would be better at it," Athena explained.

Duke walked out of the puddle. "You mean you have trouble with the test, too?"

"Sure," Athena replied. "I get caught up in my head, thinking about the best way to approach the ramp with maximum speed. But that ends up costing me time. I never finish fast enough."

"Hmm," Nova said thoughtfully. "The school isn't going to change the test. And we can't change ourselves for the test. Unless . . . "

I'VE GOT IT!!

Duke frowned. "Um, Nova, none of your ideas today really worked."

Nova shook her head. "No, this is different. Wash up, and then go find Peanut. I know what we need to do!"

CHAPTER 12

THE K-1 EXAM

"**W**elcome to the K-1 Exams for our fourth-year pupils!" Principal Finefur announced.

The students of Barksdale Academy clapped and cheered. The three younger classes had all finished their K-1 exams, and now it was time for Nova, Harley, Peanut, and Duke to compete. They waited in front of the bleachers on the school's agility field.

"This is it," Nova said, taking a deep breath. "It's now or never."

"You'll be competing in teams of four," the principal continued. She and Coach Houndstooth sat behind the judges' table at the end of the obstacle course. "One at a time, each member of the team will go through the course. You'll be judged on total speed,

and your ability to get through the course without knocking over any obstacles."

Mandy and Randy were sitting behind Nova. "Guess that means Nova will never pass the test," Mandy said loud enough for Nova to hear. Nova ignored her.

Coach Houndstooth took the microphone from Principal Finefur. "First up is a team that contains some of the school's best athletes. They call themselves Team Awesome. Come on up, Ace, Ollie, Mandy, and Randy."

"That's a cool name," Harley whispered to Nova. "Kinda better than Team Comeback, don't you think?"

"It's okay," Nova whispered back. "I thought of an even better one."

The four dogs in Team Awesome climbed down from the bleachers and lined up behind the starting line of the agility course.

"R-r-r-ready, Team Awesome?" Coach Hound-stooth asked.

"Ready, Coach!" they replied.

THEN ON YOUR BARK, GET SET, GO!

Randy took off first for the team. He wove through the cones, climbed up and down the ramp, jumped through the hoop, ran through more cones, and then pulled a rope to ring a bell at the end of the course.

That was the signal for the next teammate, Mandy. She completed the course perfectly. So did Ollie, who came next. Ace took off last, and he ran through the course so fast that he became a blur of spotted fur.

"Excellent time!" Coach Houndstooth congratulated them. "A school record. And flawless execution."

Principal Finefur flipped the scorecard for their team: **100!**

Nova's tail twitched nervously. *I guess we know which team will win Best in Show,* she thought. *I'm pretty sure my plan will work. But what if it doesn't?*

Three more teams went through the course. Some dogs knocked over cones. Athena and some other dogs were slow. One pup even tripped going through the hoop. But the teams all got good scores: 83, 95, 87.

"How many points does our team need to pass?" Duke asked.

"Sixty-five," Nova replied.

Duke's eyes got wide. "But we've never gotten more than ten points before!"

Nova's tail began to twitch nervously again. "I know."

"Next up, we've got a team that calls itself Team Underdog," Coach Houndstooth announced. "Come on down, Nova, Harley, Duke, and Peanut."

"Nova, why did you call us Team Underdog?" Duke asked as they made their way to the field. "I thought you didn't like it when Mandy and Randy called us that."

"I know," Nova said. "But I realized it shouldn't bother me. We *are* underdogs. And we're going to be the best underdogs we can be, right?"

Harley grinned at Nova. "You can count on me."

"I'm an underdog, and proud of it!" Peanut added. "Now come on, gang. **LET'S DO THIS!**"

They made their way to the starting line. First Duke, then Peanut, then Harley, and finally Nova. Nova's left front leg bounced up and down nervously.

"Ready, Underdogs?" Coach Houndstooth asked.

"READY!" they replied.

"On your bark, get set, go!"

Duke took off first. He swiftly wove back and forth through the cones. When he got to the ramp, he ran right around it!

The dogs in the bleachers reacted with surprise. Principal Finefur frowned.

"What's he doing? He can't just skip it!"

But that's exactly what Duke did. He jumped through the hoop, ran through more cones, and rang the bell.

Peanut took off next. Everyone in the bleachers gasped.

"What's he wearing?"

In fact, Peanut was wearing a plastic suit that covered him from the tops of his ears to the tip of his tail. Granny Goldenfur had made it for him. The little dog trotted along the course, moving slowly and making squeaky noises as he moved. Principal Finefur frowned again. But Peanut finished!

Ring! The bell rang, and Harley took off. Nova looked to the bleachers. Ace ran out, just like she had asked him to, holding a stick with a stuffed squirrel dangling from it. He ran in front of Harley as she made her way through the course.

"SQUIRREL!" Harley yelled, and she moved faster than Nova had ever seen her. She was right on Ace's heels! Principal Finefur frowned and shook her head.

Ring! Nova launched from the starting line.

Don't knock anything over! Don't knock anything over! she told herself.

And she didn't. She weaved through the cones. She climbed up and down the ramp. She gracefully sailed through the hoop.

"Go, Nova!" Athena cheered from the stands, and some of the dogs began to clap.

Joy filled Nova as she ran through the last line of cones.

"**I DID IT!**" she yelled, and then she jumped up to ring the bell . . .

. . . and soared right past it, landing on the judges' table!

The table knocked over with a clatter. The score-cards toppled to the ground. Principal Finefur and Coach Houndstooth jumped out of the way.

Nova landed. The joy left her. She deflated like a popped balloon.

Oh no! I've ruined everything!

chapter 43

THE FINAL SCORE

Some dogs in the bleachers started laughing. Principal Finefur and Coach Houndstooth picked up the judges' table. Nova moved to help them.

"No, that's okay," Couch Houndstooth told her with a kind smile. "We've got this. Wouldn't want you knocking ever-r-r-ything over again!"

Harley, Duke, and Peanut gathered around Nova.

"It's okay, Nova," Duke said, putting his paw on her shoulder. "You did great."

"Yeah, really great!" Peanut agreed. "Until you crashed."

"I'm sorry, pups," Nova said with a sigh. "We'll never pass now."

Harley shrugged. "That's okay. We've never passed an exam before!"

Principal Finefur faced them.

"That was quite the performance," she said. "I had to take points off for refusal to climb the ramp. Points off for unauthorized clothing. Points off for not ringing the bell. Points off for destruction of school property."

Nova hung her head.

"But . . ." the principal continued, "all of you finished the course. Your time was not bad. And you received some extra points for creative problem-solving. Here is your final score."

She flipped the scorecard: 66.

The four friends stared at the card, frozen, with their mouths opened.

"We . . . we passed!" Peanut said.

They hugged one another and began to jump up and down.

WE PASSED! WE PASSED! WE PASSED!

Principal Finefur cleared her throat. "Very nice, Underdogs. Now please return to the bleachers."

Nova, Harley, Duke, and Peanut ran back to the bleachers and sat down.

"What are you all so happy for?" Mandy asked.

"Yeah, what?" Randy added. "You got a terrible score."

Peanut hopped up between them. "Listen up, you two. We're happy because we passed. And we did it *our* way!"

Then he climbed back down and sat next to Duke.

The four friends cheered on the students in the other classes. Then Coach Houndstooth and Principal Finefur stepped out from behind the table and faced the students. Couch Houndstooth held a trophy.

"And now it's time to present the award for Best in Agility for the K-1 Challenge," he announced. "While fourth-year student Ace Swiftrunner did have the fastest individual time, we had to deduct points for his interference with another challenge."

Nova looked over at Ace. He'd been so nice to help them, but that had cost him the trophy. He shrugged and smiled at her.

"So, the trophy goes to . . . Ollie Woofur!"

Everyone clapped and cheered as Ollie rolled out to accept his award.

"Very well done, everyone," Principal Finefur congratulated. "Our next challenge will be in three weeks. Now, go enjoy some pizza, courtesy of Chef Wolfgang!"

The students all climbed down from the bleachers. Nova, Harley, Duke, and Peanut walked toward the pizza table.

Athena trotted up. "Great job, Underdogs!"

"Yeah, Underdogs, congrats!" Ollie said as he rolled past them.

Nova grinned. "I guess our name is going to stick with us," she said. "Now the Underdogs just need a plan to pass the K-2 exams . . ."

"Can't we just enjoy our victory for a little while?" Harley asked.

Nova nodded. "You're right," she said. "Who's ready to celebrate?" Nova cheered. She jumped up, pumping one paw in the air. Then she started to fall backward . . . onto the pizza table.

Duke, Harley, and Peanut grabbed her and pulled her back before she crashed into the table.

"Thanks for saving me. I don't think I'll ever be Best in Show," Nova said, but then a Granny Goldenfur–like thought popped into her head. "But you know what's better than Best in Show? Best friends like you!"

Nova held out her paw. "How about a team cheer?"
Harley, Duke, Peanut, and Nova touched their
paws together.

TRACEY WEST has written more than 300 books for kids, including the *New York Times*-bestselling Dragon Masters series for Scholastic Branches. The canine companions Tracey has known during her life have all served as inspiration for the Underdogs. She currently lives in New York state with her husband and four adopted dogs.

Kyla May is an Australian illustrator, writer, and designer. She is the creator and illustrator of the Diary of a Pug and Lotus Lane book series and illustrator of *The Sloth Life: Dream On*. Kyla has also contributed her imagination and talent to six animated TV series, as well as toys and gifts for children of all ages. Kyla lives by the beach in Victoria, Australia, with her three daughters, three dogs, and two cats.

Keep reading for a sneak peek at
We're Not the Champions, the next book starring

the UnDeRDOgS

Chapter 1
SCAREDY-DOG

Duke the bulldog panted in the warm afternoon sunshine. He watched his friend Nova walk to the end of the diving board.

"I call this move the Butterfly!" she announced, jumping up and down.

She bounced off. **BOING!** She launched into the air, flapping her arms.

Whoa, that looks scary! Duke thought.

SPLASH! Nova landed in the lake. Water droplets shot up as she hit the water. Then she swam to shore and climbed onto the grass, shaking her golden-yellow fur.

"Be careful, Nova!" cried Peanut. The little dog was stretched out on a beach towel next to Duke. "I don't want to get my fur wet!"

"You don't know what you're missing!" Nova replied, and she shook her head again, hitting Peanut with one last sprinkle of water.

"Aaaargh!" Peanut cried.

Duke laughed. "It's just water, Peanut."

"Oh yeah?" Peanut asked. "Why don't you jump in, then?"

Duke frowned. Peanut knew why Duke wouldn't jump in. He wasn't afraid of water. But heights—yikes!

"Hey, look at me!" Harley called from the diving board. "I call this one the Flipperoo!"

Harley launched off the board using her short, powerful legs. She somersaulted in the air.

SPLASH! She slammed into the water. Then her head popped up.

"What do you think of that one?" she asked as she doggy-paddled to the shore.

"I liked it," Nova replied, and she bounded toward the diving board. "I want to try it!"

Harley shook the water off her fur, and Peanut frowned.

"I keep getting wet!" he complained.

"Well, maybe you shouldn't have come to the lake, then," Duke teased.

Peanut leaned back and slid his sunglasses over his eyes. "It's Saturday! Lake Barksdale is the place to be."

Duke gazed around. Sunlight glittered on the dark blue surface of the lake. On one side was a sandy beach, and on the other side, a grassy meadow. Dogs swam in the water, dug in the sand, played volleyball on the shore, and snacked at picnic tables. The welcome sign informed visitors that Lake Barksdale was:

THE BEST LAKE FOR SWIMMING!
THE BEST LAKE FOR PICNICKING!
THE BEST LAKE FOR HAVING FUN!

Typical, Duke thought. *Everyone and everything*

in Barksdale wants to be the best. And everyone and everything in Barksdale is the best. Everyone except us.

Duke, Peanut, Nova, and Harley were four friends known as the Underdogs. They weren't the best at anything. Except, maybe, at being themselves. And that was just fine with Duke.

Nova tried to somersault off the diving board. But instead of curling her body into a ball, like Harley had, her legs spread out in all different directions. She landed on the water with a **SPLAT** instead of a **SPLASH!**

She ran out of the water, laughing. "I'm going to need some practice," she said. "Hey, Duke, you wanna try the diving board?"

"I think I'll just get my feet wet," Duke replied.

"Aw, come on, it's not even that high," Nova urged.

Duke didn't answer right away. Nova had recently tried to help him get over his fear of heights—one of the many things he was afraid of. It hadn't worked, but Duke had been proud of himself for trying.

"Weeellllll," he said slowly, "it *is* hot. And jumping in would cool me down."

Harley pulled Duke off his blanket. "You don't have to do anything fancy. I'll give you a push if you want."

"No, you definitely don't have to push me," Duke said, suddenly feeling nervous. But he followed Harley and Nova up to the diving board on the end of the dock.

Harley took off. **"THE ROCKET!"** she yelled. She bounced on the end of the board once . . . twice . . . and the third time, she shot straight up into the air. Then she landed in the water feetfirst, with her arms down at her sides.

Nova giggled. **"THE JELLYFISH!"** Nova called out, charging off the board. She wiggled her legs in a silly way as she sailed across the water.

The two pups paddled in the water, waiting for Duke.

"Come on, Duke!" Nova shouted.

"You can do it!" Harley yelled.

Duke slowly walked to the edge of the board. He looked down into the deep lake. His heart began to beat fast, and he froze.

"Nope," he said. "Just nope. I thought I could do it, but I can't."

"That's okay, Duke!" Nova told him.

Duke slowly backed up off the board—and bumped into something furry.

He turned around to see two twin dogs with floppy ears—Mandy and Randy Fetcherton.

"What's the matter, Duke? Scared?" Mandy asked.

Randy pointed. "He's a scaredy-dog!"

They started laughing, and some of the other dogs on the beach joined in.

"SCAREDY-DOG! SCAREDY-DOG!"